D1499053

Thank you—I am thrilled you are reading one of my first two historical novels of the "Journeys" series. I hope you will find them encouraging and worthy of your recommendation. I would be very interested in your comments and happy to speak to your group or book club. For additional information and to order more signed copies: www.OneWayBooks.org. All books are available on amazon.com, and your local bookstore upon request.

Sincerely, Mac McConnell, mac@way.org

BOZRA

A Shepherd's Journey to Jerusalem

MAC
McCONNELL

ONEWAYBOOKS

ISBN   978-0-9800451-0-9   10 Digit - 0-9800451-0-X
Library of Congress Catalog Card Number: 2007938192

One Way Productions—www.way.org— (954) 680-9095
Literary Agent—Les Stobbe

DEDICATION

To my wife, Linda,
without whom I would not understand,
much less be able to write,
a shred of believable romance.

ACKNOWLEDGEMENTS

Words escape me to say sufficient thanks to
Bill and Vicki Rose.
Their steadfast encouragement, unwavering friendship
and abandoned support is surpassed
only by their kindest words, "you *are* family."

Thank you,
Donna Goodrich and Jodee Kulp
for uncanny editing.

TABLE OF CONTENTS

Dedication
Acknowledgements
Foreword

Tell all the Truth but tell it slant —

Success in Circuit lies

Too bright for our infirm Delight

The Truth's superb surprise

As Lightning to the Children eased

With explanation kind

The Truth must dazzle gradually

Or every man be blind —

Emily Dickinson

FOREWORD

I ask your additional indulgence before you embark on
  this modest volume I have had the occasion to jour-
  nal over my long but simple journey. Simple? Yes.
  And yet, in no small way touched by unique occur-
  rences that should cause some astonishment even in
  the two thousand years hence.
Shepherds are a bit of an outcast. Their company fits
  best, and is mostly, with other shepherds. This only
  heightens what I am about to tell you.
I lived at a time unlike but a few.
  A time prophets dreamed of.
    A time immersed in danger and intrigue.
  A time of change.
    A time that changed me.
      And now it is time for you.

Would that I could reach out of these pages and touch
  you myself to whisper a blessing on each syllable
  you read. It will have to suffice I have, to the best I
  know how. Believing we are connected across these
  times by the words — and hidden treasures—you
  now hold.

  Bozra, son of Abraham.

ONE
The Test

I was told it was a test. It wasn't. It was nothing more than a tease. A trick really.

My oh-so-brilliant brothers decided to take advantage of their little brother on his...my...most important night.

My first as a shepherd.

It was a family tradition that I would have to learn the hard way.

My usual way.

As the youngest I had no say in the matter whatsoever. The youngest by a full six years they like to remind me.

They were not the sympathetic type.

This made me the undershepherd of Jeheil, my closest brother up the line. Then it was Gahazi the know-it-all. And Elliab who insisted on bragging about *the twins* he would say in his most masculine voice. Next was Benaial, the quiet one, with a smirk that told you nothing. Then Aaron, old enough to be my father, was always so serious, as if the whole family couldn't possibly understand how important his opinions were.

This was my big night—morning really, as undershepherds always start with the last, the fifth watch. The least trouble, the least dangerous.

I was told the others were perfectly asleep.

It was just Jeheil and me.

I was told.

Jeheil was much more than a brother to me. Come to think of it, he was just about everything to me. So I was in good hands, and that was a good feeling.

Truth is I should have figured this out, but I wasn't thinking. Completely too anxious to be on watch, all I could think was *don't mess this up, Boz boy.*

I studied everything Jeheil did. He would be leaving me soon.

Out here in the wilderness.

I watched his every move, but there wasn't much to watch. He was watching me, my every move, which was nothing more than he was doing,

not much.

It was so dark each star looked like flying embers from our campfire.

The Test

I heard every creak, every lamb, every grunt, rustle, crunch, owl,
 every howl.
Jeheil sat and leaned against the old sycamore stump.
 "Go on, Bozra, walk the herd."
I knew what to do and knew that it was time the herd
 got used to me, my smell, my ways.
A few were skittish at first, but they settled back down
 soon enough. I expected they felt safer with any one
 of my brothers.
 So did I.
I was just settling in to my stroll, round the herd, the far
 side from Jeheil, when a shudder rippled through.
 The herd bristled then froze.
 I did too.
A wild beast must be near.
I peered for Jeheil, but as soon as the noise started, it
 was done, much to my relief.
Sheep spook at the slightest, littlest ol' thing. Given
 the right circumstances a jackrabbit could send
 them into a stampede if their shepherd or sheep-
 dog wasn't right near.
With a snort, Goliath, the biggest sheepdog you could
 hope for, loped over and the sheep relaxed.
 Me too.
Goli's coat shimmered in the moonlight,
 black as a beetle's back.

The battle scar above his snout, his winter coat and piercing eyes could scare off the real Goliath. The sheep respected Goli. If they knew what was good for them. His eyes were as sharp as his teeth and he nipped their heels when they strayed or lagged too long.

It began.

"Boz."

"Yes brother, I'm right here."

"Finish up then."

I did.

"Boz, come, relax. Take my place. Sit, lean back against the stump. I need to relieve myself."

I watched as he left wondering why he needed me here to do that. I sat and leaned back with a queasy feeling that this was a big mistake.

It was.

Shepherds worth their salt seldom sat for fear they would doze. But it was Jeheil's idea, so...

I glimpsed a falling star and leaned back as it streaked overhead.

Another mistake.

As quickly as my head hit the stump my eyes slammed shut.

As quickly as that, my eyes popped open to five of the ugliest, scariest, vilest faces looking ready to pluck out my eyes and suck out my brains.

This was my worst nightmare. Then it got worse.

"We told you!"

An ungodly chorus from my ugly brothers—accented with sun rays burning my eyes and beaming between their uglier heads. My ears told me my dreaded fears had come all too true.

It happened just as they planned it.

Planned it well.

I was caught asleep just as they predicted.

Just as they hoped.

"Hey, I'm just a kid," I screamed, squinting beneath my arm. Trying desperately to block the sun and get to my feet and hide somewhere.

A terrible reply, because they would all agree. I was acting like a kid.

A poor excuse and poorer response. I had just compared myself to a kid, a goat, to their delight.

"You can't help it. You were an accident. A surprise," they reminded me again.

I came along a full six years after Jeheil and this gave them great pleasure and a constant barb to sink into my thin skin.

"No surprise to me." Another prized reply. I didn't even know what I was saying, but they laughed so hard I had to laugh too.

As the youngest by so many years I had the ridiculous duty of tending and teaching the snot-nosed children of our clan. It was more tending than teaching and made me miserable. This was a pitiful life for a soon-to-be shepherd. Some of these kids smelled as foul as the sheep, upwind, after a day of eating alfalfa. At least I didn't have to wipe the sheep. My only relief was when Jeheil joined me for bedtime stories. He was the master.

Jeheil took pity on me and my plight with his own memories of such things. "This will be perfect training for you, Boz. You will see."

I didn't see at all.

But Jeheil was all too ready for me to take his watch, so he could move on up the order with his thoughts of manhood that I already credited him with.

The little ones giggled endlessly when Jeheil finished supper and belched his way over to our corner of the tent.

They adored him and that made me jealous.

But I was as glad to see him as they were and to hear his latest yarn.

On and on he would go while poking the embers of our little evening fire. Coaxing the little ones to sleep one by one.

They listened as best and as long as they could to the
long preposterous wild adventures that happened
only in his imagination.

The flames dancing in their eyes as the tales danced in
their minds.

Then the enchanting began.

Jeheil would lower his voice, look at me, and with a
wink, move to the youngest. He sat talking soft and
low and scary.

Gently he placed one hand behind their little heads and
leaned them back.

I would stifle my chuckle as he lowered his other hand
slowly down in front of their eyes. The little head
and shoulders went slack and the little one was in
dreamland.

Just where I wanted them.

It was quite the show. Each one lulled to sleep by
Jeheil's quiet voice. We carried them to their waiting mothers.

Then wait for the watch as Jeheil would too often have
to rouse me from my own slumber.

"Bozra? Sleeping or sheeping?"
Jeheil whispered in my ear,
enjoying my startled dismay.

He started off to the fields knowing I'd fumble all over myself to catch up.

He stretched out his walk and I'd trot to keep up. I would grab his staff and hang on, trying desperately to match his stride.

I worshiped my brother. His steadiness. His wisp of a beard I envied.

As we came to the crest of the little hill overlooking our flock, Gahazi always passed us, heading back to camp without a word.

Jeheil would eye the field from horizon to horizon. I watched his gaze to see if he paused at anything.

Our home fields were the most beautiful and peaceful of the other six. These grazings had been in our family "since I can't remember when," Father said. Just one half day south of Bethlehem it felt as remote as the rest, each a day's trek in circuit till right back here on the seventh week and fresh grazing.

I couldn't wait till we left again, away from most of the children and to each new adventure.

I can't explain it. I could stare at the flock and fields for hours. There was seldom so much as a twitch of an ear on this watch.

That was what I looked for in the moonlight.

Any movement.

Jeheil said the sheep would signal us of any danger from wolves or wild dogs if we watched carefully.

I did.

"Or bears," Jeheil mumbled. I looked to see if he was joking. I couldn't tell. Bears were no joke.

"Tell me about the time you ran them off," I asked for the thousandth time.

Then the smirk.

A cocky smile. A puffed up chest.

"It was wolves, four of them..."

"I thought it was three."

"No, four. And hungry. And mean. They stalked the herd all night and kept them restless. That's what saved them and me. I knew something wasn't right."

"I started to camp to wake Gahazi, but feared it was too late for that."

Jeheil's eyes glazed and looked distant as if he was hundreds of years old with infinite wisdom and experience and battles and adventures.

"I knew if I called out, that could stampede the herd. They were spooked as it was. If I cried wolf and there was no danger I would be in big trouble, and never trusted again.

"Boz, I was frightened. My stomach knotted, my chest burned, I was afraid to even blink. I'd seen wolves rip the throats of sheep in a frenzy and knew they could rip mine too."

Jeheil grabbed my throat and shook me silly. We laughed.

He more than me.

With a snarl Jeheil went on, "Bozra, my skin crawled when I heard the low ugly growl from deep down the throat of the vicious, hungry animal." Jeheil took his storytelling seriously.

"It was off to the right of the herd. I didn't want to move but had no choice. What would Father do? is all I could think. The herd must be protected at all cost. Just one drop of spilt blood and the rest of the wolves would attack at once. The sheep would scatter every which way, the wolves would drag off their spoil, and we would be tracking down strays for days knowing many would be gone for good."

Jeheil shivered as he recounted the gory details. I wondered if he was just leading me on and smiled back at him.

"You don't think this is serious, do you, Bozra" I swallowed my smile as Jeheil snagged a nearby lamb and brought it back. He told me to sit. He laid the four month old in my lap.

"Boz, do you not wonder why we have so few sheep and so many lambs most of the year?"

"Yes, of course, but…" I had wondered, but I didn't want to sound stupid, so hadn't said nothing.

"Do you not wonder why Father inspects the lambs so
    closely?"

"Yes, no, not really. I just know he loves them."

"Good, Bozra. That's right, he does. We all do."

My brother Jeheil, my best friend, even when he sneaks
    up to scare me stupid. Or when he joins the others
    and laughs at me for sleeping on watch.

Someday I would do the same to my brother, Jeheil told
    me. "Another surprise is on its way, and due any
    day."

Father was ready for another son.

I was ready for a little brother.

Mother wanted a girl.

But I wanted, needed, a brother. If it was a girl, I would
    still tease my nephews.

  I would tease someone.

Jeheil sat beside me against the stump. He leaned against
    my shoulder, sweeping his hand out across the hori-
    zon, over the herd. "Boz, these are the most pre-
    cious lambs in the whole world."

"Of course they are. They're ours."

"That's not the half of it." Jeheil was exasperated. "It's

time you understood." I was sure this was going to be another yarn.

"Boz, that is a spotless lamb." The lamb squirmed, let out a puff and settled back. "Go ahead, see for yourself. Run your fingers through its coat. Examine for yourself, you must learn anyway."

I did as told. As I had seen many times.

I turned the little lamb in my lap. I had to turn too, as the moon was to our back. I began to sink my fingers into the young fur.

The little lamb was enjoying the rub.

I could clearly see the beauty of a spotless lamb. My legs cramped up, but I didn't care.

"Boz, a spotless lamb is our specialty, our pride. Father, the whole family, we have all dedicated our lives to this. Most sheep in this valley are not sheep at all. Most are lambs like you hold. But ours are the best, and the best cared for. Keep looking and see if you can find a blemish, a spot, an insect or broken bone."

There were none. And this was no yarn.

"You will examine thousands in your lifetime. Be very particular, for this is a special lamb."

"Jeheil, are you going to tell me why we have so many lambs and so few sheep?"

"Finally, you ask the right question. We do not raise sheep. We raise lambs."

"You can't have one without the other."

"So wise, little brother. Now think what you said. The truth is we have many lambs for most of the year. Then no lambs, nearly no lambs at all."

"I guess I never thought about it much."

"You never thought about it because you were too busy napping." Jeheil pushed me and laughed. "You were born napping."

"Was not."

"You were, too. But back to what I was saying. We only raise sheep to raise perfect lambs. This is the business of Bethlehem. Our life, our livelihood is perfect lambs. Only perfect lambs are suitable for the perfect sacrifice."

My mouth dropped.

Sacrifice? I could not imagine letting anyone take a dagger...I could not.

"Brother," I elbowed Jeheil. "Listen to me, I must keep this one. I must raise it and protect it and love it and care for it and...and never let it out of my sight."

Jeheil grinned. "You must ask Father."

"Who? Me? But what if he says no? What if he won't let me? What if he says we must sell it to be...to be sacrificed? What if, Jeheil?"

"Then you will do what he says. But don't put words in his mouth."

"You ask him for me. He won't turn you down."

"Father loves you, Boz. You can trust him, and this is
something you should do for yourself."

"But...but...Father is so strict."

"Because he wants the best for you. And expects it from
you too"

"But what if he says no, Jeheil? What if he says I can't
keep it?"

"Then you will do what he says."

"But..."

I might not be able to keep this precious little lamb.

I may not be able to protect it. I may lose it.

Forever.

My tears disappeared in the fur as I looked at this tiny
sleeping, breathing, helpless bundle.

"Bozra, one day you will feel that way about all the
sheep."

My heart thumped.

"No, just this one, just this one," I blurted. But Jeheil
only grinned and got up to check the flock.

I didn't fall asleep. I couldn't take my eyes off the lamb.

I would keep it and raise it—no matter what Father
said.

Somehow.

The rest of the watch I kept Zeor close.

I took my belt and made a noose.

That's my name for my lamb. Zeor, the bundle.

My bundle of joy. That is how I thought of this baby ram.

Father would certainly let me keep Zeor since I already named it—him.

He couldn't refuse me.

He just couldn't.

Maybe I'll just run away with Zeor, I thought. But I was already hungry when Jeheil returned.

"Bozra, go in for breakfast and bring me some."

"No, I'll…I'll stay. You go, and bring me some. I'd better stay."

"Are you sure?"

"Yes, of course, it's sunup. I'll be fine."

Jeheil left with a smirk.

I looked at the flock and my Zeor.

My hands cramped from holding the rope.

"Zeor, I will protect you." I squatted and stroked his head. He looked up at me.

I was sure it would be fine with Father.

I was.

Mostly.

I heard the crunch of footsteps and my mouth watered, ready for something to eat.

Zeor rustled,

I turned,

but it wasn't Jeheil.

TWO
The First

It was Father.

Was I in trouble?

Was Zeor in danger? Jeheil told him? I'll skin him when
I see him. I'll... I'll do something to him.

"Father? Good... good morning."

"Morning, my son. How are you this fine day? Are you
nervous about something? Scared?" Father chuckled.

"No, no, Father, I'm very well. Not scared."

"Good for you. There's nothing to be scared about, is
there?"

I wanted to say, *Yes, there is.*

> *I'm scared you will not let me keep Zeor.*
> *I'm scared you will sell Zeor and*
>   *someone will slit his throat.*
> *I'm scared I will never see him again.*
> *So, yes, there was a lot to be scared about,*
>   I was thinking.

"Father, I... I want to keep this little lamb. I have named it Zeor, because he is my joy. I will watch out for it and raise it, and it—I mean Zeor—will not be a problem for anyone. And...and I will be a good shepherd for it...him...Zeor.

"Father, I haven't asked you for anything, not in a long time, and I really need to keep this lamb, Zeor, safe and well and alive and not for sale or anything like that."

I was breathing too hard.

Father just stared at me.

For the longest time he just stared.

I didn't know what to do. I knelt by Zeor and pulled him close, ready to run.

"Yes, Bozra you can keep him."

"Father, I will be a good shepherd. I will protect and care for him and watch and feed him and he won't be a burden, a problem, for anyone and I will still do all my chores and everything."

I was out of breath.

Father was laughing. "I said yes."

I didn't know what to say. I flung myself at my father. I slung my arms around his waist. "Thank you, thank you, thank you. You are the best father in the whole world. I love you so much. Thank you, Father."

I was breathing again.

"Bozra, wipe those tears from your face right now. You are too old for that, and now you have responsibility. You will not disappoint me, will you?"

"No, no, no I won't Father. You can trust me, I can do it."

"I know, son. You will need to learn, so pay close attention to your brothers and close attention to…what did you call him?"

"Zeor, Father, my bundle of joy."

"And you are mine today, Bozra. I'm proud of you. I hope you have put as much thought into this as you say."

"Yes, Father, I have, and,

I am proud to be your son."

I was.

THREE
The Brilliant Idea

One morning,

    I was awakened during the fourth watch.

    I heard my father up and muttering as he pulled on his clothes.

We were in our home fields and something must be wrong.

As he left, I pulled up the tent and poked out my head.

    All my brothers joined Father as he headed toward the flock.

Jeheil was already there. It was his watch.

I started after them,

    but Father said, "Go back to sleep."

"Mother, where are they going?"

"Father couldn't sleep. He thinks something is after the flock. I don't know, he's been uneasy all night. Go back to sleep like he said. The flock is in good hands."

Mother went back to sleep.

I tried.

What if there was something after the flock,
    after Zeor?

        I'd better go.

Sure that my mother was breathing deeply, I pulled on
    my tunic and reached for my new shepherd's staff.

I had worked it for weeks. Jeheil helped me form the
    crook. We soaked it for hours, bent it around pegs,
    then soaked and bent it until it was just right.

I sanded and smoothed it, especially the grip. It was too
    big, "but not for long," Jeheil had said.

He gave me his rod to go with my staff. I hung it from
    my waist by a short strap like my brother did. The
    rod was for my protection, but it banged my thigh
    when I ran if I didn't hold it.

All my brothers and my father were out in the field and
    I didn't want to miss whatever this was.

As I came down from the path, I stopped, looking to see
    why my brothers and father were all here.

        I didn't see a thing.

            I watched as Father sent Benaial and Elliab
            off in different directions round the flock.

    Aaron, climbed a hill.

The Brilliant Idea

Gahazi and Jeheil moved quietly through the flock to keep them at ease, touching them lightly on their heads and rumps.

No one saw me.

I sat back on my heels steadying myself with my staff. My rod poked me and I moved it. It was too big to get my hands around, *but not for long.*

I looked and looked but all my brothers were back now with Father.

Some sitting, some standing. Just talking.

Jeheil had gathered some branches and added to the campfire. I couldn't understand what they were saying, but it didn't sound all that important.

I hoped Mother was still asleep. She must be, or she would be after me by now.

I slipped up to the mound to listen out of sight.

But they were still just talking.

I leaned against the little hill and laid the staff across my waist. I took the rod and wound the strap around my wrist as I was taught, in case of trouble.

It was a mistake to sit.

That is, to lean back against the little hill.

I had been up late with the little ones and then had snuck out to check on Zeor once already.

My eyelids sagged.

I kept saying to myself, "Bozra sit up, stand up.

You will get caught and disappoint Father. Your brothers will yell at you and everyone will have a good laugh and they will never trust you with the whole watch by yourself."

I rubbed my eyes but they were too heavy and burned now. My whole body felt like a big old log.

Sleep.

I slept. Like a big old log.

And the nightmares started. My brothers yelling in my face over and over, "We told you."

Sure enough.

Worse than any nightmare.

Light blaring, burning my eyes.

I blinked. It stung.

Sun?

Can't be.

Yes. Somehow I had slept through the entire watch.

I could not believe it.

Father will be so disappointed. I was mad.

How could I have let this happen?

I grabbed my staff to stand, but something was strange.

The light was everywhere,

coming from everywhere.

I knelt to peer over the little hill, wondering if I was only dreaming.

There they were. My brothers—all of them—and

The Brilliant Idea

Father, and Goliath, staring at the sun, the light. The
light filled the sky, bright and beautiful. It made my
family shimmer. They were just standing and staring,
looking all aglow in the light—shining.
I started to run to them, but the light started to fade and
that stopped me.
My mind was spinning.
Father and brothers, all of them, turned and rushed
right at me.
The light was gone and they were in a hurry. Goliath
trotting behind them.
There must be great danger.
Or this was a gigantic trick.
I tried to look around them to see what all this was
about.
"Bozra, get ready!" Father practically screamed as he
brushed by, apparently not surprised to see me.
"Get ready? Ready for what, Father?"
"For town. We're going to town." Father started off
again. I started after him.
"To town? What for?"
"To see the baby." Father was all excited about some-
thing as we all headed to camp.
"Baby? What baby."
"Just get ready."
Nothing made sense. My brothers were ahead. Goliath

33

was with them. Bethlehem was a nice little town, but we rarely went there unless someone was deathly ill or we were out of something we couldn't do without.

I tried to think.

No. No one in all our families was with child.

For a change.

Besides, we never went to town to have a baby that I knew of. And who would watch the sheep?

That's when I had an idea.

A brilliant idea.

"Father. Father wait." We were at camp now and there was much commotion. Father stopped and looked down at me.

Not pleased.

"Father, can I stay and watch the sheep? Can I, Father? While everyone goes to see this baby? Someone should stay and watch the sheep and I could do it."

Father stared at me for the longest time.

It made me nervous.

"Alright Bozra, you can stay."

"I can do it, Father. I can do it. You can trust me. I won't fall asleep, I won't. The sheep will be safe and I will be safe. You can leave Goliath with me, too. You can go to town and not worry about anything. I will be right here on the job. I will be very careful. I can do

34

it. I'm old enough and there is only the fifth watch left." I stopped to breathe.

"I said alright, Bozra. You can stay and watch the sheep."

He had said alright. He said yes. He started toward our tent.

"Father, what was that bright light and where did it go?"

Father stopped. He turned around and knelt on one knee in front of me.

"Bozra." Father placed both hands on my shoulders. He looked me right in my eyes,

"I thought you heard, Bozra."

"Heard what? Did...did someone die?"

"No, not at all. Bozra, the most wonderful thing has happened. The Messiah is born this day in Bethlehem and we have been invited to go and see him. And you should come with us to see this wonderful thing."

"No Father, I want to stay, to watch the sheep." I wasn't sure what a messiah was, or if I needed to see him. Father stood, smiled and scruffed my hair.

"As you wish, son." He turned back to our tent, took his cloak and started off.

Mother was already ready and everyone started toward the Bethlehem road. Even Goliath. I watched as Jeheil held up a finger and told him to stay. Goliath's head drooped. He sat and watched them off.

I watched, too.

Goliath came dragging back and licked my hand. They were all gone now. There was just me and Goliath and Aunt Anna who stayed to look after the little ones.

I went to the fields.

It was quiet and dark.

It was still and cold.

I looked to see if anyone had come back, but no one was there.

Just me and Goliath and the dark and the cold and the still.

I wondered if maybe I should have gone to Bethlehem.

I wondered if I might be missing something.

This morning seemed longer than most.

Goliath slept a lot. I did not.

Not even sit. Squatted back on my heels, that was all.

I made rounds and walked through the sheep. The ewes and rams and lambs were at complete peace.

Zeor was, too.

In just a few hours I felt all grown up.

I finished rounds with Goliath at my heels.

I imagined this was my flock, my sheep, my lambs.

I thought about having a family and boys and a herd and a dog all of my own.

"Someday I will be one of the shepherds of Bethlehem. King David was a shepherd, maybe at this very spot, I shall be, too." I declared right out loud.

Someday.

Then,

the most beautiful sight.

The sun was edging up over the hills just the other side of the valley full of our sheep. A heavy dew wet the grass and the herd. A mist drifted undisturbed.

Sunbeams began streaking through the trees on nearby hills.

Then the beams became sharp and straight. They split the fog and mist and made the dew on everything glisten and sparkle.

I stared.

Goliath sat up perfectly still and stared, too.

The more I looked, the more there was to see.

The whole sky was all lit up.

The trees looked ablaze.

The colors were like a giant rainbow, only spread out flat along with the dew and filled the mist with a glow.

The clouds were full of color too. Sunbeams shot around and through them and streaked skyward in great bands of light that fanned out far and wide.

I looked hard, not wanting to miss anything.

Then it was over. A flock of doves darted through and it was over.

The sun went white hot.

The mist was gone and the fog was too.

The dew was drying, the flock was stirring, the chill was over. Goliath trotted off to do his business.

I knelt to thank Jehovah for this wonderful sight. I got back up and was suddenly aware of my stomach growling.

I wondered if my family was ever going to come back.

I wanted them to see I had done it.

The whole watch, and then some.

They would respect me, and be proud of me.

I was proud of me, but hungry too.

I forgot to pack anything, and knew better than to go to camp and leave the sheep.

Goliath barked.

They were back.

Finally.

"Bozra, come, we have wonderful news." It was Aaron, but I wanted to tell them my wonderful news.

"Bozra, come listen. We saw the child. He was beautiful, and born just at sunrise." It was Benaial, but I wanted to tell about my sunrise.

"Bozra, we met Yoseph and Mary and little Yeshua." It was Gahazi, but I wanted to tell them I had done the whole watch and then some.

"Bozra, come now," Father said. "I'm very proud but you look very tired. Here, get some breakfast and we will tell you all about it, and about the angels."

I was tired and hungry and now speechless. Angels? No one told me there would be angels.

I did miss something very special.

I wondered if this messiah they all seemed to be so happy about was kin to us.

"Who will watch the flock?" I said.

"Goliath," someone answered as everyone laughed. True enough, Goliath would let us know if there was any danger.

They told me of their trip into town and the family from far away that had the baby.

They told me about the angels that visited them in the fields.

They were full of joy,
   and too much wine,
      as far as I could tell.

I ate and listened to their unbelievable stories, wondering if anyone appreciated what a fine job I did while they were away having so much fun.

One day,
> my thirteenth birthday,
>> a cloud of dust rose up and it wasn't another
>> herd of sheep.

I looked to see the most magnificent caravan. We all
stood staring.

I ran, Goliath at my heels.
> Who, what could this be?

From the cloud emerged three camels, with feathers—
plumage Father called it—on their heads.
> And braided manes. And embroidered reins.

Riders swayed lazily on jeweled studded saddles.
> Just behind came more camels and carts. Servants
> and beautifully covered wagons with swags of cur-
> tains swinging back and forth.

Then, animals I never saw before.
> Large.
>> Big as mountains, with long snouts and huge

ears and whitewashed all over.

"Elephants. Look at the elephants," Father said.

Look? Who could not look?

Like walking mountains they were, that someone painted white.

"Look at the oriental carpets." Father was more excited than I remember since the day of the angels—the angels that I didn't see.

"If angels came to see us then this royal caravan is coming to see us too." I hollered.

That made Father howl. "Sorry, Bozra, they're probably on their way to see the boy Yeshua."

I was sure these men were kings or something.

Someone special. Royalty I supposed.

Heavy beautiful robes and fancy shoes with toes that curly-cued back.

Their language sounded as foreign as they looked, but one spoke our Aramaic, asking many questions.

Before I realized what was going on, the servants pitched a tent, placed pillows and cushions all around. Then they invited Father and Aaron to enter and sit.

Suddenly, there were more servants with baskets of fruits and nuts and dates and I don't know what all.

I was drooling, as they poured juices and water and wine from ornate jugs and pitchers.

The Visit

"Bozra, offer our stream.

Help water their animals."

The excitement broke as Father sent me to help even more servants tend to the animals. It was obvious from all the smiles, the nobles were very pleased.

I must admit they had fine animals, the whole lot of them.

Then,

I got to pet the big grey mountain.

That wasn't all. Three servant boys dressed only in loincloths and beautiful head wraps showed me something amazing.

One grabbed the elephant's long snout and pulled it around his waist.

He slapped the snout two times, and like being caught up in a whirlwind, the elephant swirled the boy out and around and up and plopped him on its back.

I let out a gasp fearing the boy would be flung away.

They all giggled. I couldn't help but laugh too.

"Can... can I do that? Will you let me do that?

Can I get up on that big thing?"

I asked before thinking.

They did not understand a word I was saying, but my waving hands told them exactly what I wanted to do. So two of the boys, one on each side, took my arms and pulled me along.

I looked to see if my father was seeing all this, but he was busy with the nobles.

The boys—Egbar and Jabed they called themselves— brought me to the front of the huge animal.

Their grips on my arms tightened when I stepped back, and they giggled again. Their eyes were bright, and their smiles were as big as their faces.

I suddenly wasn't too sure about any of this, but before I could resist, Egbar reached out with one hand to take the big long snout and wrapped it around my waist.

It was hot and rough and a little too tight. I had to catch my breath.

With another two slaps from Egbar—or maybe it was Jabed—the next thing I know, I was spinning and upside down and flying, and thump, I was sitting on top of the mountain. Then the third boy—called Bekmid—stood behind me clapping his hands together and slapping me on my back.

Egbar and Jabed also jumped up and down and hollered something that sounded like approval.

Holding on to the big rolls of grey-white skin, I was wondering what came over me that I was doing this, but so very glad I was.

A roar came from the tent, and I looked to see them all clapping. Father looked amazed, his hands clasped over his head.

The Visit

Then Bekmid slapped the back of the elephant. He
motioned to me to slap its head. I did,
without thinking

Bekmid slid behind me and grabbed my belt, as we
started to move. My grip tightened so hard my
knuckles went white.

Moving with great rolls and lurches, I was sure I would
fall, crash on my head and die. I was afraid to look
around.

Then the elephant stopped with a lunge, his two front
legs in our stream.

Just as I thought I was safe, he stuck his snout deep into
the stream.

I saw the big snout aimed right at me.
Like a waterfall it was.
Hins of water gushed all over me. I ducked from the
water as Bekmid stood up, but too late and he got
drenched too.

This was a great way to get a bath whether I needed it
or not.

Then I heard another roar from the tent. Everyone was
laughing. I had to laugh too, it was so unbelievable.

But I held on tight.
Bekmid crawled over and around me and slapped
the big elephant's head.

Ka-thump.

The elephant dropped to his knees. I grabbed all the skin I could grab.

I watched in horror as Bekmid disappeared.

Splash. Bekmid was sloshing in the stream.

I knew I was next.

I looked, and just as I suspected everyone was watching and waiting for me to join Bekmid.

A grin stretched across my face as all of them waved their hands urging me to slide down.

Gripping hard, I said a prayer. Before I could change my mind, I thrust forward.

I let go too late. Head over heels I rolled. Down the snout, into the stream, straight to the bottom, banging my head.

When I surfaced, gasping for breath, I barely noticed the gash on my head. I didn't care.

The elephant was spraying everyone with water. All the servants were jumping into the stream and Goliath right in the middle of us all.

The nobles and Father came to watch. They congratulated me for my death-defying performance.

"That's enough, son. We need to let these nice people go now." Father reached out a hand.

"What is this?" He dabbed at the blood.

"Nothing, Father, nothing at all. Father, where are they going?"

The Visit

"Just as I told you. To Bethlehem to see Yeshua."

"Through these fields? Where did they come from?"

"Well, many places they told me, but through Jerusalem this morning."

"Why through our fields, through Jerusalem, then to Bethlehem? Did they get lost? Such an easy journey."

"No, Bozra. They aren't lost. They just prefer to stay off the main roads, and told me this was a surprise, and for us to tell no one."

"That is not going to be easy, Father."

The servants began taking down the tent, and others loaded up all the things they had gotten down from the carts and wagons.

Father took me to meet the nobles. With big smiles and squinty eyes, they presented tiny ivory elephants in beaded bags to everyone.

This was the grandest day of my life. The best birthday of all.

I said goodbye to Egbar, Jabed and Bekmid and the most wonderful animal in the whole world.

While wringing the water from my clothes I had an idea.

A brilliant idea.

"Father, I can go with them? Can I, Father? I want to go with them and see Yeshua. I know the way. I've been there before. I'm of age. I know the way back. I know they will let me come with them. I won't be any trouble. Father?"

This was a brilliant idea.

"Bozra no. Sorry, but no. We have lost a whole morning's work and you have much to do."

"But … "

"No buts, Bozra! You know better than to press me when I've said no. Someday you will see Yeshua."

Father was right.

I did know better than to press him.

I could have gotten a whipping.

But I was so disappointed watching them leave.

Dust rose from their carts and wagons and animals.

Bekmid was still waving.

I wasn't going with him.

I wasn't going anywhere.

And I wasn't going to see Yeshua this day.

Soon,

I wondered if someday would ever come.

FIVE
The Prayer

"He should have been back hours ago."

Mother was a fret, reminding Father over and over. "Where could he be?"

Jeheil had gone to town for needed supplies and was long overdue. Dusk was creeping in.

I was supposed to go with him, but overslept. Then Mother sent me to chop firewood we didn't need today at all.

She was worried sick, but if Father was, he wasn't letting on.

"All right, I'll go find him," he said.

"Can I go?" I thought this would be the perfect time to go to Bethlehem.

"Yes, get your things."

Mother hurried to gather coats and staffs and skins of water.

I was ready, but...

Goliath barked.

We turned to see Jeheil entering the camp.

I wasn't going anywhere.

We rushed to see him.

To see if he was all right.

Mother just stood and stared, fighting back tears. Father put his arm around her, she buried her head in his chest, and looked back at Jeheil.

Aaron, Benaial and Elliab went to Jeheil but Jeheil started to moan. *What would make Jeheil act like that?* I wondered. He looked like he would collapse.

Then I saw blood on his clothes. Everyone else did, too.

Mother started to sob. If Father hadn't been holding her, she would have sunk to the ground.

As best she could, she made her way over to Jeheil and threw her arms around him. He steadied himself with his staff. Father tried to see where he was injured, but Jehiel just shook his head no.

Father got him something to drink from the dinner tent, and water to wash his face and the blood and dirt from his hands.

We went and sat and waited around the table.

There was nothing I could do.

Nothing any of us could do but wait.

I could not imagine what I would hear.

All my life I had lived here with my family and sheep and never had to worry or be afraid of much. And now to think that my brother was in trouble or hurt.

I wanted to make it better, but I couldn't do anything and that made me even more upset.

Jeheil choked, and then he looked at all of us.

"I have something awful to tell you," he began. His face flushed, and he dragged the back of his hand across his nose.

"I went to the Bethlehem market and was in one of the shops." Jeheil stared down at his cup. "Joram was helping with the supplies. I had just asked him if he knew if Yeshua was still in town, when we heard it. It sounded like thunder." Jeheil looked away. He had fought off wolves and bears and such and now could barely talk.

Father reached across the table and put his hand on Jeheil's arm. "Go on, son. We're right here with you." Father's voice sounded shaky, too.

I wanted to say something. Do something. The suspense was horrible.

Finally.

"I stepped out on the stoop to see what was going on, and saw Roman soldiers on horseback. They were everywhere in full gallop coming our way. They stopped in front of Joram's shop, kicking up dirt and rocks everywhere."

Jeheil took a deep breath.

"Merchants and shoppers came outside to see, but

quickly retreated when the officer barked orders and the army scattered in every direction. Joram grabbed my arm and yanked me inside. I wanted to go back outside and see, but he said it was too dangerous.

"For hours we hid in a small dark closet with shelves of supplies on all sides, and I did what Joram said—pushed and piled seed bags in front of the door.

"I'm glad to hear that, Jeheil." Father was more calm now. We all were, as we got used to the idea that Jeheil was all right.

Jeheil took another drink. "We heard a crash in the shop, we knew the soldiers were inside. I tried to see Joram, but it was black as mud in there. We heard them kicking things over and shouting, but the little room made everything muffled, we couldn't understand a thing they said.

"Joram and I were holding our breath. The banging was loud and once it was right outside when the door swung open. Then cursing, and the door slammed shut, knocking the seed down on us. I could feel the air go right out of me." Jeheil took some more water.

"Take your time, son. We're not going anywhere," Father said.

Mother got up and sat by Jeheil. She took his hand up to

her cheek, and then held it in her lap. She looked stronger now.

"Then it was over," Jeheil went on. "We heard the soldiers galloped off. Joram and I got up, moved the bags out of the way. He peeked around the door and we went into the shop. It was torn up—a mess. Stuff, clothing, seed, tools and crates had been kicked and thrown from one side to the other. We didn't know why. Joram told me to take my things and go, as we saw his strongbox busted and empty."

Jeheil grimaced, remembering. "Outside I saw what all the screaming was about. Families were sobbing in the street. Blood was splattered everywhere and little babies...little babies dead...in their mother's arms."

Jeheil was practically shouting now. Angry.

He started again, slower. "The mothers' clothes were covered with blood. Blood on their arms and down their dresses. People were just walking around in shock. I walked through town, back up the road home, trying not to look at everything. It was so unbelievable and sad.

"I was practically dragging myself from the town. Then I saw a dead baby in front of a house. Someone's poor dead baby—lying in the dirt, lifeless and bloody, facedown and shapeless. I heard wailing from the house, and somehow, I managed to pick up the limp body and take it inside.

"The mother was sitting in the corner sobbing, with her head on her knees, rocking back and forth. As I knelt beside her, she just looked up. Slowly she reached for her child and began to rock again, weeping all the more with her head buried in the baby."

I could mostly see everything Jeheil was saying.

"I sat by her with my hand on her shoulder." Jeheil put his hand on Mother's shoulder when he said that. It was not the best idea as she shivered a little.

Jeheil went on. "Finally a neighbor came in, and I just got up and left. Now I'm here and I don't know what happened or why."

No one moved.

"Father, do you...do you think they killed Yeshua?" I said.

"I don't see how they could not have, Bozra. I don't see any way, barring a miracle, that he could still be alive."

I went to the fields.

Helpless.

To think...all those little babies.

Then it came to me.

The Prayer

If our fields were on the north side of Bethlehem, those
soldiers could have come right by here.

We have babies.

My little brother and my nieces and nephews.

I sank to my knees, holding my staff. Looking up I
prayed,

"Heavenly Father, thank you my family is here and safe.
Thank you my brother is back. Father, I hope, I pray,
little Yeshua escaped somehow. I want to see him. I
never got to see him. Please protect him. He needs
one of your miracles."

I thought on those things I missed, and now I would
never know the meaning of it all.

I went back to camp as night closed in.

Father was alone.

Oil lamps flickered in all the tents. It was oddly still.
Somewhere a nephew or niece whimpered.

It was a wonderful sound.

I took my covers in our tent, and laid down with my little brother. Again I thanked my God as I pulled the
covers over us in the chill of the night.

It was time for me to be more responsible, more grown
up. I surely didn't feel much like a kid anymore.

This was the longest day of my life.

Zeor was busy, a productive sire and my little flock began to grow.

Something else grew.

My love for my little lambs, if not the whole herd.

I was proud to be their shepherd, even when one ran off and got lost or became a tangled mess. Sheep love to tramp off on their own I guess, or they're a bit too dumb to know any better.

Odd, how you can be attached to an animal that's so interested in itself. I have watched a lamb follow its nose, chewing the clover right off the edge of a ridge, then bleat for help and look up with expecting eyes as if to ask, "Where have you been?"

No matter how many sheep and lambs I would ever own, if one wandered off, I wouldn't rest until I had it in my arms and back in the fold. Even Father was surprised at my strength from lifting so many to safety.

Just as Jeheil told me years before, as I blubbered over

little Zeor, I would love them every one.

I would give them everything. Protect them at all cost.

They would give me nothing in return.

Well, that's not true at all. It just seems that way when one after another made me chase after them, or have to scrub them time and again because they don't bother to stay out of the muck.

I was well shed of tending and teaching the children and spent most of the day in the fields while still keeping my watch. Now the fourth.

They were my love, passion, center of attention, until...
Until...Leah.

SEVEN
The First Wait

She walked into the fields one day
    and confused everything.

Her hair was tied off in a light blue scarf or it would
    have reached her waist, at least.

It flopped with each step as she picked wildflowers one
    at a time and pushed them into the bunch she held
    in her left hand.

Uncle Zebb told us his cousin and family were coming
    for a stay, but he didn't tell us about Leah.

    I don't think.

      I don't remember.

        I must have missed the part about Leah.

My new sheepdog, Junior, from Goliath's first litter,
    still a pup, a big pup, looked up at me. Then trotted
    over to her, slinging his hopeful tail.

He was glad to see her too.

    Leah was startled for just a bit, then reached over to
    pet Junior's head. This wasn't easy because he was
    busy licking her hand.

That's when she looked at me.

 And I didn't look away.

The best I remember,

she was petting Junior, half bent over, when she stood...and looked right at me, again.

Then she gave a little wave and turned and started briskly back toward camp. The dust of the field swirled behind in her wake dancing and sparkling in the sun.

I felt a little like that too.

I can't explain it.

I wanted to leave the field for something other than food and yet my stomach was achy. Like I needed to eat, but I didn't.

She was the most beautiful thing I ever saw. I began to doubt anyone could look so...

so beautiful.

Strange new feelings rushed through my body,

but I didn't seem to mind. I never thought something, someone, could confound my little world so quickly.

I stayed out there all that afternoon.

Kept looking back at camp, hoping she would come back, but she didn't. I began to wonder if I saw her at all. I began to wonder what was wrong with me.

I waited for this day to end so I could go to dinner and

see this wonderful thing.

It felt just like the time I asked Father if I could keep Zeor.

> The same childish feeling,

> > but strangely eager, and manly.

That night at dinner I waited till everyone was at the table, and saw there was a place next to her on the end.

I heaped too much on my plate, trying to look at ease.

When I came, she reached down with her left hand, the one she had held all the flowers in, and pulled her dress out of the way.

I sat down,

> but I was looking at her instead of where to sit.

Before I could grab anything, I was sitting

> in the dirt,

> > my dinner in the dirt as a great roar rose from the table.

Leah was giggling so hard she had tears in her eyes. She tried to stop the gasp of laughter escaping between her fingers held up to her mouth.

I thought about crawling under the table but I started laughing too. I couldn't stop as everyone—including Leah—were standing and applauding my great feat of grace.

I got to my feet, took a bow, then went for another

plate. Goliath and Junior and the whole pack gobbled the feast I left on the ground.

Returning with dinner number two, I looked at Leah. Grinning, she waved me back to try again.

I was real careful, and before we knew it, everyone else had left.

We were alone.

I had no idea what to say, so I just ate—can't remember what, but I ate it.

Leah watched.

I was pretty sure whatever was wrong with me, was wrong with her too.

We didn't talk much.

Not at all.

We stared a lot.

Then,

"You will have to ask Jareb," she said.

"Jareb? Who is Jareb? Ask him what." I wondered if I had a rival already.

"My oldest brother. Father died with the fever and Jareb is head of the family now."

Her voice was a bit breathy. It was…I don't know how to explain it. I just wanted to listen to it for the rest of my life.

"Ask him what?" I repeated myself.

That's when she, Leah, got up and stomped off.

The First Wait

I started to follow, but Father's hand was suddenly on my shoulder and he sat me down.

To explain things.

And that was a good thing, because I was feeling pretty stupid what with dropping my dinner and sitting in the dirt and all, and with Leah getting up and leaving like that.

"Son, we need to talk."

"Father, can it wait? I need to go see what Leah is doing."

Father put his hand on my shoulder again, and I sat down, again.

That was a long night.

Father told me all kinds of things I had never thought about.

About girls and women and ladies and families and even bigger responsibilities than sheep and lambs and sheepdogs.

He told me that he had already spoken to Jareb, and if I wanted to court Leah it was all right.

"Father, she's all I can think about."

"Good, son, I imagine she feels the same. You are old enough to have your mind on something other than your herd and Junior. Don't be in such a hurry. But maybe you better go tell her."

"Tell her what?"

"It'll come to you."

I thanked Father for his advice, but I wanted to tell him
I wasn't sure anything was going to *come to me*.
Leah was waiting…sitting on a fallen palm tree by the
water's edge, dragging a stick in the stream. My
heart pounded. She was so lovely.
I put my hand on her back.
I didn't want to scare her.
She barely moved. Not scared. Just straightened up
and slid over a little and I sat by her
till my bottom went numb.
We stared at the stream and the stars and the moon—
and each other.
"Leah." A shout from camp.
"Who's that?"
"It's Jareb. I have to go. Will I see you tomorrow?"
"I think so, yes." *If I live that long*, I thought.
And she left.
In the moonlight.
Skipping.
Swaying back and forth and humming.
I'll not forget that night. The night I loved something
besides sheep, and dogs, and family.
Leah,
Leah,
Lea-a-a-ah.

EIGHT
The Worst Wait

I only thought I was nervous when I met Leah. But when the wedding day finally came I was in a panic. And my brothers did all they could to keep it that way.

Father tried to keep me calm, but not very hard. He was amused at the whole thing.

Mother's interest was on Leah, "I will finally have my daughter," she said every day for months.

All the women doted over the bride, I could hear them snicker when I passed her tent, which I did at every chance.

I haven't seen Leah all week. Stupid tradition if you ask me. Stolen glimpses at most. It kept me sick to my stomach. Or was it the summer wine? My brothers were delighted at keeping my cup filled.

The morning of the first day of the wedding feast I awoke.

Sunlight blaring in my eyes.

This was not right. I distinctly remember going to sleep

with a tent over my head. The next thing I see is five faces screaming, "We told you." They hadn't told me anything for years but the memory was all too fresh.

My ugly brothers had managed to pick me up, bedroll and all, take me outside and wait for me to wake. My head was already pounding, but we had a good laugh.

They more than me.

I had no idea what time it was, but I was sure I should be getting ready for my big day. A bath, a shave, my hair cut, my betrothal clothes. New sandals from Nat the cobbler would arrive before noon. A gift I needed desperately. Sandals without crusty dung in every crease.

I will finally see Leah. More than just see her! The next five days we would feast and dance and sing and eat...and eat. Each family prepared enough food for all of Bethlehem. But I had more than eating on my mind. In five days we would be alone—if I lived that long.

The anticipation had me yearning, aching, about to scream. I was hopelessly in love and angry at every minute I had to wait.

"Bozra, Zeor has ripped your wedding robe." My head jerked around to see Jeheil holding a lump of shredded cloth. I snatched the rags and wondered if I should have sacrificed Zeor long ago—then felt ashamed. Zeor had been neglected and no doubt was seeking revenge, but still, we could always have more lamb for the feast.

"Boz, relax." Jeheil was laughing. I had been the butt of yet another joke.

"Enough!" I screamed, a command for all to hear. "Enough!"

I left for the stream, escape. A bath. Surprised at my own wrath.

Cooling off was what I needed in more ways than one, but I forgot to bring clean clothes. My special day was starting horribly.

I picked up a stick and traced circles in the water. Leah. From that first day, eight months now, she was more than I could hope for.

I practiced my vows once more, which I had done on Junior for weeks.

I imagined Leah's face in the ripples, captured by my words. I would make her proud and my brothers envious, if I thought of them at all.

Hearing the musicians beginning to tune their instruments, I turned and saw Jeheil. He had followed me to pull something I was sure. I gave him a little shove. He must've been off balance or I was stronger than I thought. I left him sitting, spitting and slap-

ping the water. He was a sight.
A good sight.

With great patience I began to dress. I made it a ceremony. A king dressing for his queen. Leah would be
dressing now too with much more to fuss over. I
thought of our long strolls and her weightless walk.
She did most of the talking at first. Most of what I
tried to say just showed my ignorance of ladies and
life. She never noticed. She would just put her delicate finger to my lips and smile as if I didn't need to
say anything at all. She made me feel like a giant and
a gnat at the same time.

She thought our first kiss was her idea.

We were beneath the almond tree on a sunny Sabbath.
A long walk from camp. I laid back. Stretching my
arms and folding them under my head, my eyes shut
to the flickering sunlight between the leaves.

I waited.

Then, more like a dream—a soft, moist, delicate, warm
pressure on my lips. This was not a dream. But it was
all I had dreamt about, longed for, and planned for
weeks.

She was staring back at me with sun streaming through
her hair and making her whole head shine. An angel

had just kissed me. I breathed in her breath and closed my eyes, satisfied to die right there.

I started to say something, then she kissed me again. I didn't need to say something. That said it all.

I looked at her. At her blushing cheeks. Her eyes glanced down, then up. I sat up and wrapped my arms around her. Then I pulled back, cupped her face and kissed her. Her eyes burst open. I was feeling so strong, every muscle in my body ready to defend this angel, this flower, this...

"You will marry me, Leah." I should have said, Will you marry me, Leah? But...

"Yes," she said so quickly as if I didn't give her any choice.

She had said yes. It felt like a lifetime ago, but was still clearly etched in my mind. And now, in just a few hours—more like an eternity—we will be together forever.

"Son." Father entered the bridegroom's tent, quickly his raspy cough returned. Uncle Zebb was with him, my best man. Uncle Zebb was the reason Leah was here; he would always be my best man. They were both dressed and ready.

Father coughed again and cleared his throat. "It must be

the camas. I'll be fine in a few days. Are you ready, Bozra? Are you prepared? Do you know your vows?"

I was delighted. Father more nervous than I? Strangely that made me calm. I was really going to marry Leah. I will finally know what it is like to be whole. Uncle Zebb and Father had given me instructions all week.

"A man is only one half. Born to long for his other half. God's design from the beginning. Eve was taken from Adam and then given back to him," Uncle Zebb said with reverence.

"That is why you ache my son," Father added. "Leah is part of you, the missing part, even now. You have been missing her before you knew her."

That they knew what they were talking about, was obvious.

Father spoke with great authority, and I began to understand why he always put my mother first. He would scold anyone who treated her with the slightest disrespect. The worst whipping I received—the memory still stinging my mind—was the day I dared to sass my mother. He sent me to apologize. I was happy to. She smiled a little and cried a little and held me tight. "It's all right Bozra," she said. But the look from Father that day said otherwise.

The Worst Wait

Uncle Zebb passed Father and hugged me. Father was
next.

"I'm so very proud of you, my son."

"You just love Leah, Father." We both agreed, laughing it
off. But it made him choke as he sat to catch his
breath.

The camas wasn't even in our fields, but Father said,
"Any wind could pollute our pasture."

I gave Father some water. He drank slowly, then rose
with a big smile and left. "I'm fine, son, don't worry."
But I did.

Father had retreated to his tent early every night for the
last month. Sometimes not up for breakfast.
He didn't complain,
whatever this was, was worse than he let on.

Jeheil and the rest would be preparing the wedding
tent. The thought gave me a chill, but Uncle Zebb
said, "I will make sure they will do it right. No
tricks"

My stomach suddenly churned. Anticipation. Little
waves at first, then stabbing hunger. Of course. It
was a day of fasting for Leah and me. Our personal
Yom Kippur, Day of Atonement. We would be for-
given today of all our transgressions, and made holy
for our vows before the feast at twilight.

"Uncle Zebb? Where is...who will have our plate?"

"I told you, I will have the plate and your cup. Do you have your text prepared? Better let me have that too. You need only bring your heart—or does Leah already have it." Uncle Zebb grinned.

What was left of my heart began to race.

The calm was gone.

I thought it through again. The plate will be broken. With one stomp. An act to signify our engagement cannot be changed, just as the shattered plate cannot be put back together. The cup also to be broken to end our ceremony, and to begin the feasts. I will destroy it to remind us all of the destruction of Solomon's Temple that broke God's heart. Our marriage will, in some small way, mend it.

I had studied the text the whole month. The rules. The traditions. The words became so personal but made me wonder, will I ever be pure enough to wear the white robe, to deserve Leah?

My studies taught me more than I expected. I was reminded of how precious the Word of our God is and should be. I had my marriage to thank for telling me how important even this little family was to the Creator of the universe. The scriptures told me that our wedding was a divine command, a holy union. I didn't feel very holy with the thoughts of lust that delighted me. I hoped that Leah was having the same trouble.

Jeheil had relieved me of my watch this week, but I would come and walk through our herd with Junior close beside. He seemed to understand.

"You will get through this and soon wonder why you were so nervous. You will laugh at yourself for being so sentimental," Jeheil said one morning with his usual confidence.

I knew they were all laughing at me. But I knew they never loved as I do now. Being the youngest, they called me spoiled and pampered so I worked twice as hard. They forgot I had beaten two wolves to death with my staff and rod and buried them myself as a notice to any animal that thought they could attack on my watch.

I would protect my herd at all cost and now my family-to-be as well.

Besides, I was certain, all I felt for Leah would last my life. If I lived that long.

I thought about the morning of the sunrise when Father and family rushed to Bethlehem—my first full watch. I walked to the same spot. No sunrise compared to that one in all these years. Only the beauty of Leah came close. I could close my eyes to remember the colors and splendor of that morning. It would warm my face, then my thoughts would turn to Leah. The courage and confidence my father instilled in me was solid, but I was coming to this marriage with so little. A few sheep. A ragged tent. A dozen hides. A sheepdog. New sandals. Would my strength and hopes and dreams be enough? They would have to be.

I cursed my doubt.

Leah was a gift. An undeserved, indescribable treasure. How could I imagine a God so generous to just a shepherd, with little more than a heart of mush?

"You can do anything, Bozra," she told me often. I believed her too often.

I wanted to deserve her, to deserve that gleam in her eye. I wanted to confess that I could never live up to who she thought I was, but she might agree.

I will doubt but not give in, I told myself. She loves me and that will sustain me. I will be the man she wants. She needs. She deserves.

I will.

"Bozra, Bozra." A shout from camp startled me. "Your father. He's. . .he's fallen." Leah? She shouldn't be there. She shouldn't be calling me. Seeing me. I bolted and ran to her. I stumbled to a stop when I saw the anguish written all across her face.

"Bozra, I'm so sorry." She wrapped her arms around me
and I saw the others waiting by the tent.

"Come," was all she said, but I ran ahead.

Mother was by Father's side holding his hand in both of
hers. Her eyes were closed as she prayed softly,

"Not now, dear Lord, not now."

"Mother, Father, what?"

"I'm sorry son. Go on with your wedding and know
that I am with you and so very proud of you."

His voiced cracked and trailed off.

Then I saw my father's head slump.

Mother screamed...

She collapsed on top of him sobbing.

I stood in shock.

Filled with unbelief.

Terror.

Anger.

This wasn't real at all.

Suddenly everyone pushed by me. Leah's hand rested on
my shoulder. Then she took my hand and slowly
turned me around.

"They didn't want to tell you how very sick he was. He
didn't want anything to spoil this day for you...for
us."

"Well, it did."

Now Leah looked shocked. I was surprised at my words, my thoughts, when it hit me. Father is dead! I sank to my knees, dragging Leah with me. All our big plans sank with us. I knew Father was sick, but he hid it from me well…or had I just ignored it?

Go on with the wedding?

Unthinkable. How could I think of the celebration and first night with Leah? It was gone. Vanished. For the first time I can remember I was furious with Father. And I was angry at God. How could this be happening to me?

Just unbelievable.

Everyone thought I was in grief because of Father. But my grief was for me. Someone should have warned me. We could have easily moved the wedding up a week—a month.

Now what?

"Bozra." It was Uncle Zebb. "Bozra, we will have to wait for the wedding."

As if I didn't know this.

I left.

As Father wished, we separated the herd so each family would have their own flock and each field in rotation. We soon appreciated the wisdom of that decision. Although I was haunted by my feelings for him the day he died, and apologized to him often, I was strangely at peace as I clung to his last words,

Know that I am with you and so very proud of you.
I was determined to keep it that way.

The hurried wedding was less than we imagined, but the marriage night was much more than anything I could ever dream of. I flush at each thought of wonder, of such an experience. Such splendor.

I was more than glad our marriage hut was far removed from the camp. Breakfast was left at the front of the tent, but the food was dead cold by the time we bothered to retrieve it. Leah stroked my leathery skin, aged by all my extra hours with the sheep. Her skin was finer than any baby I had ever changed. I'd better cease with this or I should spend the day with Leah and forget the herd altogether. And Jeheil could not have been more wrong. I will never regret the worry or the feelings I had that day.

Leah finally recovered from giving birth to our second child—another son—and we knew there would be no more.

Junior was all the help I had with the growing flock so we pitched our tent close to the field while the boys grew.

Each seventh week all our families and flocks gathered in the home fields. There was just enough room and it took all of us to clean and inspect the sheep and lambs.

We had hours of work, but a wonderful time together, laughing and singing and talking and eating while our children spent their time waterlogged in the stream. I hoped someday they would see an elephant.

We often talked about the day of the angels and the caravan and the awful experience Jehiel went through in Bethlehem.

We often worried and wondered about Yeshua. But life as a shepherd was a hard life and kept us all concerned with the matters of everyday.

The News

Aaron, my oldest brother, became too frail to travel, and we decided to keep some family in the home fields all year round.

It was best as the growing number of sheep and shepherds was alarming. More and more merchants from Jerusalem came oftener for lambs. Our fields would be overrun with strays and shabby herds if someone wasn't there full time.

Lambs—sacrificial lambs, the business of Bethlehem—had the town teeming every year now. Just last season we had joyfully helped build a small temple for our itinerate priest, Rabbi Rhokhim.

One Sabbath, when we were in the home fields during the Feast of Unleavened Bread, we went to temple. The whole family and children over ten. Our custom at the end of holy week each year.

This year, Rabbi Rhokhim was joined by three unfamiliar priests who seemed overly anxious to greet everyone.

It looked like the whole town had come. Some of the men, actually many men were strangers as well.

Our wives and young children climbed the narrow steps to squeeze into the balcony already bulging with women and children.

We pressed in the best we could and some of us were
    separated.

The smell of incense filled the crowded room.

The sun streaked through the smoke, giving everything
    a mysterious look.

The chatter swelled as many tried to outtalk each other,
    apparently trying to impress all the strangers that
    we weren't such a small town.

But we were, and I preferred it that way.

One of the rabbis sounded a long low blast
    on the shofar to call the morning to order.
    I was glad things calmed.

Rabbi Rhokhim took a scroll from the cabinet with his
    usual display of tribute.

He kissed the seal and pulled the cloth mantle off Torah.

As he placed the scroll on the small lectern we—the
    men—pulled our tallits up and on our heads to a
    chorus of "Blessed are you our God, ruler of the
    universe, who makes us holy with commandments."

We kissed each side of our prayer shawls as our rabbi
    began with the blessing of the Word of God.

"Blessed are you oh God, King of the Universe, and
    blessed is your Holy living word."

Rabbi Rhokhim unrolled the scrolls to the day's reading
    from the words of King David.

The News

May those who wait for You not be ashamed
    through me, O Lord God of hosts;
May those who seek You not be dishonored
    through me, O God of Israel,
Because for Your sake I have borne reproach;
    Dishonor has covered my face.
I have become estranged from my brothers
    And an alien to my mother's sons.
For zeal for Your house has consumed me,
    And the reproaches of those
        who reproach You
            have fallen on me.[1]

Rabbi Rhokhim rolled the scroll, replaced the mantle
    and kissed the seal once more. He then placed the
    scroll in the cabinet, closing the doors to echoes of
    Amein, Amein, Amein.
Next, Rabbi Rhokhim ushered one of the visiting rabbis
    to the platform and his colleagues stood, one on
    each side as he began. "Blessed are you oh Lord our
    God, King of the Universe." Again a wave of Ameins.
    "My dear friends I have grave news from Jerusalem."
This was the last Sabbath of Passover but the rabbi was
    not referencing the scripture as anticipated.
I suddenly missed Father. How he loved temple.
The rabbi cleared his throat and pulled his beard. "Just

three days ago our temple grounds were invaded by rabble rousers and a man preaching against Moses and the Law." He squinted his eyes from the incense, or was he angry?

Growls and grumbles and hissings spread throughout the crowd. I was shocked at the outburst and looked up to Leah. She had her hand to her mouth looking at me in wonder. The sweet reverence of our temple was sadly missing.

"The man was from Galilee." More grumbling. "The man destroyed the marketplace, driving out our elect merchants."

Hissing and spitting.

The men on the lower floor raised their fists for a fight and began sweeping their feet, kicking up dust side to side looking at each other in disgust.

I felt like I should be doing the same.

"He also made belligerent charges against our temple rabbis and our high priest contradicting the prophets."

Now the men were yelling and shoving and swaying. We were all so jammed we were caught in a drove of pushing and bumping. I thought we should leave, but knew everyone would see. It would be a shame for us to leave before the final prayers and hymns.

"This man made a stampede of the lambs and kicked

over the tables of the money changers. And he busted dove and pigeon cages."

Sounds of horror and gasps and anger erupted. Many shouted out, "Who is this man? When will he be punished?"

Rabbi Rhokhim stepped up on the platform, and raised his hands to calm the crowd, with little effect.

The commotion spread to the balcony.

The people of Bethlehem are a docile lot.

Then I saw that it was the strangers who were leading this disruption in our little temple, and urging the rabbi on.

"The scoundrel escaped, but not until he had blasphemed our temple during the Passover."

Now the crowd was becoming incensed. The strangers began ripping the cloaks from their chests, and some of our townsmen did the same.

I looked to the balcony. The children and most of the women had left. I was glad.

"Who is this blasphemer? Who is this blasphemer?" The angry chant continued while all the rabbis pretended to shush the crowd.

I was anxious to hear who this was. If one man could do all this and escape so easily he must be a giant.

We heard the name...

"Yeshua. Yeshua.

His name is Yeshua."

The crowd erupted again in shouts and threats and dis-
belief. I stood there with one thought on my mind.
Yeshua.
The time is right.
It could easily be the same Yeshua the angels told
about.
Yeshua, the boy the nobles came to see.
Yeshua, who should have been killed in the massacre,
here in this city.
Yeshua, the one I didn't meet.
My thoughts soared from bewildered to excitement.
Yeshua is alive.
Finally it was time to leave. Many stayed, however, as
the strangers were making such a fuss, no one want-
ed to miss a thing.
One of the strangers reached for my staff stacked at the
door. I grabbed his wrist, and he released it.
No one will take my staff!
We left and quickly went back to camp.
No hymns.
Nothing to sing about.

The News

"Leah, I'm going to Jerusalem to see about our lambs."

"Bozra, they are not your lambs anymore. You just want
to find Yeshua.

I thought the flock needs be moved…"

"Leah, I need to see for myself."

"What if he is not who you think?"

"Leah, I'll go straight to Armi's. He will know. He's my
best customer, he will tell me what happened, and it
will be good for business. It will only take me a day
to get there, a day there, and I'll be back on the
third—two days before we move the flock."

"Who will go with you? Jehiel?"

"He has his hands full and this is something I have to do
myself."

"Oh, why do I bother?" Leah started toward the cup-
board. "Wait, just a minute, I'll fix you a satchel
with something to eat and drink.

Give our best to Armi, and here, take a jar of honey for
dear Cena."

"Hurry home husband."

Leah slapped me on my tush as a reminder that
she would be waiting for my return.

TEN
The Trip

The road to Jerusalem was crowded with travelers leaving the Holy City, most headed back to Hebron miles south of Bethlehem. Some I knew. Some customers, and some that used to be.

Merchants were leaving with their carts of trinkets and souvenirs swinging from straps and hooks as they distanced themselves from Jerusalem. The food wagons were empty, clay pots clanging as they passed with flies buzzing at the scraps imbedded in the cracks.

The dust had me coughing the whole way.

Just south of the city, I could see the gold glistening from the top of Herod's temple. It had been under construction since I can't remember. I was thrilled with the thought of the completed temple and so regretted I did not bring the family.

The crowds stiffer now.

Passing Hinnom valley, I covered my face from the stench of the burning refuge piled high.

The road from Bethlehem brought me in past Herod's
gaudy palace through the Gennath Gate. I turned
south, crossing the bridge that led me west of
Huldah Gates and into the court of the Gentiles by
way of the Royal Porch.

I stopped to cool my thirst, and to catch my breath after
rushing up the steps leading to the Temple Mount.
I was sad to see the Court of the Gentiles strewn
with debris and remnants from the thousands upon
thousands of pilgrims who had come to do business,
fill their purses, and make their annual sacrifice.

Dust and litter and trash were being blown about by little whirlwinds.

One lone tent with tables, lying on their sides, remained
as a reminder of the events just past. Even the mas-
sive marble columns of Solomon's Portico were
filthy with soot from smoke and ash of countless
lambs slaughtered and roasted in the huge caldrons
now charred inside and out.

The drainage troughs for the sacrificial blood were
dried and crusted. Crows and pigeons pecked at rot-
ting remnants.

It was hard to imagine that this was holy ground.

No priest in sight.

I went on to Armi's shop in front of his home near the
Sheep Gate north of the temple wall, and was wel-

comed with many hugs and kisses. The youngest child held hands high for me to hoist her on my shoulder. A wonderful aroma assured me I was just in time for dinner—lamb shank with mushroom sauce and carrot stew.

I didn't realize how hungry I was, but quickly remembered what a wonderful cook Cena was.

The wine—cool and delicious—nearly made me forget why I was here.

I was hesitant to ask, but after dinner, as Cena collected the dishes and cleared the table, and the children were shooed outside, I couldn't wait any longer.

"Armi, some rabbis were in Bethlehem yesterday and they told us…"

"About the man Yeshua?" Armi was sneering while swirling his wine.

He knew what I wanted to know.

He knew I wanted to know what he knew.

Armi shook my shoulder.

"Bozra, come, let's walk. Cena, we'll be back."

He hooked his arm through mine and we strolled along the north wall. Armi greeted a few along the way as he puffed his pipe filled with Turkish tobacco.

"I traded one measly lamb for two omers of this wonderful tobacco, Bozra. Cena likes the smell, 'but not in the house,' she insists. "Will you join me?"

I shook my head. I didn't have my pipe or the time to waste, wanting to hear what Armi had to say. He may not be as serious about his lambs as I, I understood, it was his business, but he was known to be a shrewd businessman.

"So what did you hear? What did the rabbis say?" Armi's voice was low, secretive.

"Well, we were determined to go to temple," I began. "The family was in for the week—for Passover of course. We were surprised to see so many at our little temple, strangers and visiting rabbis we had not seen before."

"Bozra, what did they say? Did you have your readings?"

"Yes, of course."

"What scripture?"

"What? Armi, you know what scripture. It is read everywhere on that day, every year, the close of Passover. From King David."

"'For zeal for Your house has consumed me, And the reproaches of those who reproach You have fallen on me.'[1] Is this where your rabbi concluded?" Armi sounded smug.

"Yes, of course."

"Bozra, come this way through the grove." Armi leaned in, talking barely above a whisper.

"Bozra, if you could've only seen what I saw," he continued. "I was shaken and thrilled at the same time. It was the first day of the Feast, and I had just gotten to the court to begin organizing my booth. When I finished penning the lambs, from out of nowhere came shouts and bangs and thuds, and then the screaming. I turned to see doves and pigeons flittering to freedom in a cloud of feathers. Then the panicked bleating of lambs and the press of pilgrims against our booth."

"Who was it?" I stopped and pulled Armi around to face me with the one question on my mind.

"Just wait. Keep walking. Don't draw attention. We don't know where this is heading yet." Armi's face was smiling, but his words were not.

"Are we in some kind of danger?"

"Not us. Not yet. But somebody is."

He ushered me along and laughed out loud for no reason when we passed a group of students. We turned back toward the Pool of Bethesda in sight of Antonia's Fortress.

"Now listen closely, I don't wish to repeat myself. Just nod and grin as we walk and talk."

"As you wish." I agreed and cocked my ear to catch every word.

"As you know my booth backs up to the temple, close to the slaughtering stalls. I was far from the commotion and had time to send Cena home with the children. I moved closer and was astounded to see one man—just one man—moving through the crowds, kicking over tables, yelling, sweating, shoving and slinging a whip. One man, Bozra. Just one.

"Who? What man? He had a whip?"

"Just wait. They must have thought him possessed or something as they all backed up, tripping all over themselves. He kept moving through the merchants.

"One after another he confronted them. His sneer dared anyone to challenge him. Boz, I have never seen such anger in the court, and wondered who would stop him, if anyone could stop him.

"Listen to this...keep walking...I saw him stomp over to the money merchants. He grabbed a table, flipped it over right at them."

"Armi that's amazing. What happened?"

"I thought this was a good time to leave when Caiafas and Nathan and Nicodemus and a whole bunch of them came rushing by. Nathan was steaming, his face more flushed than usual. He was spouting off his gibberish, showing off and pointing as if he was the only one who was concerned about anything. Caiafas and Nicodemus were conferring about something. I kept my distance but could see they somehow managed to distract this man from further turmoil in the temple area."

"Armi, was it Yeshua?"

"Ehhh, please don't say his name so loud. It is not wise."

"Armi, forgive me for interrupting, but did Yesh...did the man preach against Moses and the law?"

"He didn't preach at all."

"But that's what they said. The priest said he preached and that he caused a stampede and blasphemed the temple. Did he, Armi?"

"No. Well, not exactly."

"What does that mean?"

"He scattered the lambs and kicked over tables of the moneychangers. He even shoved people out of his way, but stampede may be an overstatement. I heard no blasphemy. He only quoted from Isaiah for all to hear." Armi leaned over to fasten his sandals speaking softly, quickly.

"He said, 'My Father's house is a house of prayer. You are a bunch of robbers.'"

"Are you telling me the truth? He called the merchants robbers? What happened then? Were they arrested?"

"Of course it's the truth, I was standing right there. As far as arresting, that is the oddest thing, Bozra. As they were standing and arguing with him the temple guards came up, but when they turned around, he was gone. Disappeared in the crowd."

"What did everyone do?"

"Most just left. Merchants scurried, trying to find their lambs. Others tried to make order out of the mess. The priest stood for a moment waiting for Caiafas to do something, but there was nothing to do. I took my lambs back to the house and we did our business there. It was a good decision. The best year I have had in I don't know how long."

"Have you seen him again?"

"Once. He was right here at the pool. Bozra, I saw with my own eyes. He was right out in public teaching, and Bozra, he was healing all kinds of sickness and illness."

"What are you saying?"

"You heard me, he was. I saw it."

"Then why are we whispering? Why aren't we shouting? And where can I find Yeshua?"

"Bozra, shush, no one is sure what to do. The priests have turned against him. They even sent some of their underlings from house to house warning everyone to stay away from the man or they will not be allowed in temple. Yeshua left, we don't know where he is. Some say he went to Bethany. Same say Capernaum."

He stopped then asked, "How long can you stay with us, Bozra?"

The Trip

"I really need to go back tomorrow. Leah was anything
   but delighted with me coming here after the ruckus
   at our temple. And my flock must move to the south
   pastures before any of our ewes lamb again."

I was convinced this was the same Yeshua I have missed
   time and again.
I'd never seen the holy city like this and was ready to get
   home.
Cena insisted I eat a huge breakfast. She packed my
   satchel with too much food and filled my skin with
   fresh water mixed with a splash of wine.
   I left.
   In a hurry,
   but stopped.
   Looked back and said right out loud,
"Someday I will meet Yeshua. Someday. I will tell him I
   prayed for him and Jehovah answered my prayers."
I had missed something very important,
   again.

ELEVEN
The Plan

Many tales circulated of the miracle worker that many
called a magician and charlatan.

After I told my brothers about my meeting with Armi,
they made every effort to tell the children all about
the angels and seeing the baby Yeshua. I told them
about the nobles and the caravan and showed the
tiny carved elephant Leah kept for me in the beaded
bag.

The more we told the stories, the more I wondered if I
would ever see him.

My brothers loved to remind me about that night I slept
through everything.

I couldn't blame them, but was plenty tired of it.

We made plans for Jerusalem, to go the next year for
Passover, but a hard winter—the hardest I remember—took its toll on the flock. It was all we could
do to make ends meet.

We lost three of our best ewes and many, many prize
lambs. Oh, how we missed Father.

My boys were getting lesson after lesson about the stubborn and selfish sheep, and about their staffs. Time after time they had to rescue a sheep from a deep wadi or flash floods from the steep mountains.

Leah kept me up to date on the latest news and some gossip as well, but one story had me wondering if she had gotten into the Passover wine.

We had just come in for a meal, after helping a new, perfect lamb, come into the world.

"Leah, what is it?" She was awfully busy cleaning.

"Bozra, my cousin was just here."

"The one from Bethany?"

"Yes, Johanna, that's the one."

"How is she?"

Leah grabbed my arm. "She told me something unbelievable."

"Then don't believe it. You know she likes to talk."

"You're thinking of Beatrice, right here in Bethlehem."

"Sorry, what did Johanna say that was so unbelievable?"

"She said that her brother-in-law Lazarus died."

"Why is that so unbelievable?" I was too tired to see how serious Leah was trying to be.

"Will you let me finish, please? Bozra, she said the man Yeshua came and raised him from the dead."

"Wait now. Wait just a minute. Raised him from the

dead? Are you sure that's what she said? Are you?"

"Yes, that is what she said and I believe her. You said Armi told you a man named Yeshua had healed many in Jerusalem."

"Healed, yes. Raised from the dead, no."

Of all the stories—we had heard plenty—but never anything like this. No one ever claimed to raise anyone from the dead.

"Leah, I'm going to Bethany first thing in the morning."

"Are you sure? Should you be gone with new lambs just born?"

"You're right. I'll start tonight. 'Aleb, get your coat and get ready.'"

"Wait… Oh, what am I saying? Let me pack you two something for the trip. I'm sure Aaron will help if needs be."

There was a hostel just four hours out. We would stop for the night and be in Bethany before midday.

I asked a shop owner, "Sir, have you seen Yeshua?"

"Seen him? Everyone has seen him."

"Can you tell me where he is?"

"No, guess I can't, he's *been* gone."

"Well, do you know where Lazarus lives?"

"Just follow the crowd."

We did. People were swarming around his porch.

Lazarus was sitting on a bench.

Looked fit to me.

He began answering questions, one after another.

"What's it like being dead?"

"Why did Yeshua bring you back?"

"How do you feel now?"

"What will you do now?"

"It's just a trick."

Quiet.

That statement startled everyone, and everyone turned
to look at who said it,

I did too.

There he was.

The people around him backed up a bit so all could see
who it was,

and who it wasn't.

A Pharisee dressed in all his regalia. Dingy grey and
black coat and shawl, fur hat pushed back, curls dan-
gling in front of his ears, his beard reaching his
plump stomach.

He rose with effort and repeated, "I said it's a trick."

Now everyone looked back at Lazarus. But instead

Martha, his sister, stepped forward holding a wooden
spoon with a towel slung over her shoulder.

"A trick?" She crossed her arms. The spoon wagging.

"Yes, you heard me…"

The Plan

"How is it that you say it was a trick?" Martha pointed her spoon, practically spitting her words. "You were here. You saw the whole thing. Lazarus, my brother, was dead alright. I myself prepared his body and anointed it with the herbs and spices. The mourners were here. Half of Bethany saw him placed in the grave and he was there three days before Yeshua came and raised him from the dead before our eyes. What will it take for you to believe?

You're not from around here, are you?"

Many joined Lazarus's laughter as the old Pharisee wandered off alone muttering.

That was all I needed to hear. Seeing Lazarus was all it took.

I will meet this Yeshua, and make sure my family does too.

Back home I gathered Leah and the boys, "Passover is now six months away. We must do everything we can to make sure all our business is finished before then. I want us all to go as a family. If the herd doesn't sell in time, we'll take what's left to Jerusalem and sell them there."

We agreed.

TWELVE
The Hope

We faced another tough winter, but we were better prepared and lost only a few sheep—a few young ones.

My oldest was courting and getting serious with betrothal expected any day.

Leah was beside herself thinking about a wedding in the family and thrilled to be going to the city for shopping at the best time for bargains.

Jeheil and Gahazi agreed to take our sheep after the Passover rush. We melded our herds as I wanted to take my family to Jerusalem for Passover without the worry of business. My boys and I—mostly the boys—picked a lamb for our family sacrifice. Leah and I had shared the lessons on Moses at our Passover meal so the boys understood the need for a spotless lamb for the perfect sacrifice.

At the last minute Aaron had trouble with his flock. Many had scampered off in the night and it took us all nearly two days to round them up.

With the late start I decided we would leave that afternoon and stop at Bethany. We felt confident Leah's
cousin would not refuse us and had the added anticipation of Leah and Josh, our youngest, seeing
Lazarus, a man back from the dead.

When we came to Johanna's, however, her house was
filled with others thinking the same. She offered us
her room, but Leah wouldn't hear of it. So we bor-
rowed a tent and pitched it at a campground north
of the city with scores of other travelers.

Our tent was large and fully enclosed with the sides tied
off. Leah arranged the bedrolls and the boys fed our
lamb, fixed a place for him with some hay and tied
him to a stake. They pulled a leaf of the tent over a
low branch for cover he didn't really need.

They were getting too attached to him, I knew.

"What should we name our lamb, Papa?"

I wasn't ready for this question.

But I had an idea.

"Boys, this is a special lamb. A lamb for God to call his
own. I think we will let him name him for us." Leah
glanced at me, impressed I had a suitable answer so
quickly.

We knew if the boys named the little lamb, they would
not be able to offer him for sacrifice.

The Hope

After dinner, the boys cleaned up and I strolled over to the campfire where the men gathered for talk. Some had come from Jerusalem and some were going there tomorrow as were we.

I hated that we lost the two days.

I wanted the family to spend more of Holy Week in Jerusalem, but at least we were here.

I could hardly wait.

"Gentlemen," I spoke and they looked. "I wonder, did any of you see the man Yeshua in Jerusalem this week?"

"See him? The whole world saw him. Have you not heard?"

"No, we just arrived from Bethlehem. Tell me. Tell me everything."

"You better pull up a rock; there is a lot to tell." They laughed, and I did too, mostly to disguise my excitement.

"The first of the week is when it started," a big man began as he moved closer to the fire. "Many of us wondered if he was going to come at all. He didn't last year. The priests sent word throughout the city that if any of us see him we should tell them. But only a scoundrel would do that. We knew they were looking for any excuse to arrest Yeshua if and when he came to Jerusalem for Passover."

Not everyone at the campfire agreed with this man, but
he was so large they didn't give him any argument.
He gained confidence as he talked.

"I was here in Bethany. Yeshua and his bunch were at
Lazarus' house for a couple of nights. On the first
day of the week they started towards the city. As
they began, two of his followers brought a young
colt up from the city. I could see them place coats
on the donkey and Yeshua mounted.

"Before I thought much about it, some began shouting
out hosannas and hallelujahs.

"Soon they were singing 'Blessed is he who comes in the
name of the Lord' as we made our way toward the
city.

"Still a good distance from the Golden Gate, I saw people flooding out of the city, rushing up the road.
They had—listen now—they had palm branches in
hand."

I couldn't understand all this, what the man was describ-
ing, but I knew I had missed something very important.

Another man stood just behind me and picked up when
the man paused. "Some began to lay the palm
branches on the road in front of Yeshua's donkey.
The children were running and playing, the people
were singing and dancing. You could hear tam-

bourines and flutes. Then they started taking their coats off and laying them in front of Yeshua. Others were waving their palm branches shouting and singing 'Hosanna in the highest.'"

I looked at each face and the face of the man who was talking. I could only think, from everything I knew, this was the kind of welcome reserved for a king.

I must have missed the event of a lifetime, when another interrupted. "Then when Yeshua went to the temple area..."

"Wait, wait let me tell this, I was there too." A man on the other side of the campfire stood up and pressed his way forward. Everyone wanted into the conversation.

"When he came to the Court of the Gentiles, the merchants, the buyers and the sellers were very busy. The noise was deafening. Then the shouts of 'There he is. Isn't that that man Yeshua?'"

"I climbed the base of a pillar, and there he was. As soon as Yeshua entered he surveyed the whole of the courtyard."

The man swept his staff in a large arc across our heads as he spoke. I had to grin, he was so excited. Jeheil would appreciate all these storytellers I was sure.

He went on. "There were many with him. It looked like he wasn't going to do anything for a moment and I thought that he had turned to leave. But he turned back. A scowl hardened his face as he started toward the market area. Those he passed were turning to watch and many followed at a distance. Someone grabbed his sleeve but he jerked it back."

"I saw that too," someone offered.

"Let me finish! I heard a man yell out, 'Here he comes again,' and I could see merchants scampering to collect their lambs or doves or trinkets. But before anyone even thought of stopping him, they began yelling warnings across the courtyard and yelling for the guards."

"Did you see how many were with him?" a man standing by me asked.

"It was hard to tell, the court was filled. Most were just stunned and stood watching as Yeshua made a beeline for the moneychangers. Two merchants stepped in front of him but with one wave of his arm they gave way. The moneychangers were busy raking in their coins but they were too late. Yeshua kicked one table, then another and another and he yelled 'Get out of my way.' They did, they had no real choice, and the coins went flying everywhere. He picked up dove cages and smashed them to the ground. The birds flew while hordes snatched up the money and stuffed it in their purses. The moneychangers were having a fit."

"Tell them what he said," someone shouted. The speaker paused, thought and continued.

"Yeshua climbed onto a table with a broken cage still swinging in his hand. He squeezed the cage and lifted it over his head and we all backed back. He looked disgusted and through gritted teeth, 'I have told you before, now I tell you again, It is written, my house will be called a house of prayer, but you are making it a den of thieves.' With that he tossed the broken cage and what was left splintered to pieces.

"Then as soon as it started it was over and he was gone. He and his followers left, going back the way they came.

They must have left the city,
I don't know where.
I was only there to pick up my lamb."

Many began to add this and that, but I was convinced I had missed everything. Everything. Again.

Back at our tent the boys were sound asleep and Leah was stitching up one of their coats.

"Did you meet everyone in the camp?" Leah teased for me being gone so long.

Our little lamb was breathing easy, oblivious that this was the last night of his life.

BOZRA

It had been too many years since I had been to Jerusalem with a Passover sacrifice.

I knelt by the lamb, stroked its head...feeling a mixture of joy and dread. We would all have to think on our transgressions and seek forgiveness and atonement through this innocent lamb sleeping so peacefully, reminding me of my first little lamb that I worked so hard to save from this very fate.

I stood and walked to the side of our tent for a clear view of the holy city. The sun was sinking and quickly bringing a chill. The silhouette of the temple walls were outlined by torches that burned all year long. Fires in the streets and on rooftops cast dancing shadows, making the city look alive. A shofar sounded signaling the end of the day's sacrifices with Shabbat just twenty-four hours away.

We had only one day to see all of Jerusalem.

It wasn't enough,

but would have to do.

Tomorrow I'll see Yeshua, and my family will too after long last, is all I could think, and that thought would keep me awake this night.

THIRTEEN
The Shock

A heavy mist made it colder than we had prepared.
Our lamb broke loose sometime during the night.

    The boys had a time finding him

        we thought it a miracle

        he wasn't stolen and sold.

We closed up the tent,

    doused our little fire

    and started the short trek to the city.

        Not much to say.

            Much to think.

We were excited, but I feared it would be too much to
    see and do.

Leah had her list of essentials. Her cousin had helped
    her with what to buy and how much she should pay.

The odors of so many visitors—mixed with smoke and
    incense layered in the morning fog—stung our
    noses as we approached the city.

Harlots were leaving the city, and guards began kicking
    the beggars sleeping by Herods' palace to rouse

them and send them on their way. Leah tried to hide
the boys' eyes. They had never seen anything like this
and Leah didn't like it at all.

The closer I got, the farther away the temple seemed. I
didn't remember it like this.

We began to hear ugly sounds as we headed to the
Gennath Gate. Tourists and pilgrims poured out of
the city; it was hard to get out of their way.

I wondered where all were headed.

I drew my family in close and told Aleb to pick up our
lamb before it ran away again.

The noise was getting louder, closer.

I wanted my family to enter the Beautiful Gate facing
the Kidron but we were already late and Armi
would be wondering where we were.

When we turned north of the western wall the noise
became shouting and cursing.

Streams of people poured out of the Sheep Gate, many
headed our way yelling "Get back! Get back!"

Why, I couldn't imagine.

When we finally reached Armi's, his gate and shop were
locked up tight, and we could hear cries and the
crack of a whip just around the corner.

Nothing, readied me for the shouts of
    "Crucify him"
    that we heard over everything.

The Shock

The crowds formed lines on each side of the street waiting for something,
What, I could not imagine.
All I could think was, This is nothing short of outra-
geous to have crucifixions during Holy Week.
Then the soldiers forced back the crowd with swords
and shields, knocking many down as they laughed
and cursed and moved on. Some in the crowd
cursed back from a distance and waved their fists
when they knew they could not be seen.
Another crack of the whip made us look.
   A criminal fell to his knees, and then facedown as
   the crossbeam slid off his back,
      leaving bloody gouges.
         The soldier kicked him, spat,
         and told him to get up.
We could see another man staggering under the weight
of a cross as the crowd mocked him.
I was mesmerized as Leah yanked at my coat, screaming.
   "Bozra, Bozra, what are you doing? Let's go!"
We had never witnessed anything like this. Leah was
right. It was time to leave.
We gathered our boys and left to more shouts of
   "Crucify him,
      crucify him,
         kill him, kill them all."

We had to walk the gutter in all its filth to bypass the
  crowds. Aleb was holding the lamb which was trying
  its best to kick to freedom.

"Just let him go." I said.

We would not be sacrificing today, the last day of
  Passover. The lamb darted up the bank and disappeared quickly. I wished this day had never begun.
  It was slow going as we tried to ignore the noise and
  shouts and cursing. Leah was holding the ears of our
  youngest and Aleb was covering his. But nothing
  could block the ugly sounds droning in my head,
  some saying one thing, some another.

"Kill him."

"No, no spare him."

"Away with this man."

"No, that's my husband. What will I do?"

"Just scourge him and let him go."

"Imposter."

"Fraud."

"Trash."

"Scum."

"Crucify him."

"Yeshua, Yeshua."

I stopped.

The Shock

I looked at Leah wondering
    if I heard what I heard.
"Bozra, hurry, we must leave while we can."
"They shouted, 'Yeshua,'
    Leah. They shouted 'Yeshua.'
    Could it be that they are going to crucify Yeshua?"
"The children!" She looked at me
    like I had lost my mind.
I was wondering the same.
    "I must find out if it is Yeshua."
"Bozra."

And we moved on.
I walked backwards hoping
    I could see something
        that would make some sense.
            I was so close.

FOURTEEN
The Meeting

We made our way back to Bethany.

The boys were still holding the rope from the lamb when…

the sun dimmed.

It went dark in the middle of the day.

We could barely find our way up the road.

I turned to stare at where the sun should be as heavy clouds sailed across the sky. A cold wind blew up a dust storm, stinging my face before I could pull up my scarf.

Leah wrapped her coat around the boys, pleading with me to hurry.

The wind moaned through the tents and tossed ashes from the campfires everywhere. Clothes flapped fiercely on lines and broke free to fly away, rolling along the ground and clinging to tents.

Chilled to the bone, I clutched my coat tight to my neck, trying to act calm and hoping to find our tent in one piece.

Two stakes were out but quickly replaced and Leah took
the boys inside as rain pelted the tent and me.

I stood on the lee side of the tent shivering from the
cold and a fear that would not go away.

I prayed, not knowing what to say or what this all
meant.

Anger swelled inside of me…at myself. I didn't know
why.

"Bozra," Leah called. I could hear the doubt in her
voice. "Bozra?" Again she called.

"Yes, I'm here."

"Please come inside, you will catch your death."

"In a minute." But I knew I wouldn't. I walked to the
front and opened the flap.

"Leah, I'm going back."

"Don't be ridiculous. Come inside."

"I'd be ridiculous if I didn't see for myself."

"See what?"

"See what I've been looking for all of my life. Yeshua."

"Bozra, it's too dangerous. What about the boys? What
about me?"

"You know I have to go." I pulled the tent flap back and
tied it off. Then I stood and put my hand on the tent
and asked Jehovah to protect my family as my dear
wife wept softly.

"Leah, I'll be back, please don't worry."
    Nothing.

The Meeting

Then, "I love you, Bozra. Please, be careful."

I started back down the slope in the darkness—feeling
  unsettled for leaving my family, and a fool if I didn't
  go.

Just as fierce as the wind began, it calmed to nothing at
  all and the rain stopped.

The sun beamed back making me squint. It had been
  two, maybe three hours.

The heat from the sun was indignant—indifferent—but
  the warmth was welcomed.

I was lost in thought.

  Nothing seemed to matter.

I was too old, had lived too long, done too many things,
  gone through so much and somehow now it didn't
  make any sense.

Had I done anything that would make a difference?

  Would anyone care that I lived?

Of course Leah and the boys and the family,
  but outside of that?

I tried to make a family—a respectable business—to
  honor my faith, my God.

I tried to do what was right, what Father had taught me,
  taught us all.

I knew I had missed something, many things, important
  about this man Yeshua,

    that many called Messiah.

That many called an imposter.

But, I didn't know what to make of it all.

And that drove me back to the city.

I grabbed a man, "Do you know where Yeshua is? Did
    they crucify him? Where can I find him?" He pushed
    me away and looked at me in disbelief and pointed.

"The skull. Golgatha. Where else?" was all he said and I
    went in the direction he pointed.

No one noticed as I moved against a sullen string of peo-
    ple, looking blankly ahead, moving quickly away.

A group here and a group there would stop and look
    back and up.

It took all I had to climb that little hill in fear of what I
    would see.

When I neared the top,
    three crosses stood alone.

The bodies had been removed but the horror remained.
    Streams of blood stained them.

        Torn flesh hung from them.

            The smell of death surrounded them.

One lone Roman horse tore at scarce tufts of grass.
    Groups of men and women huddled in sorrow.

Soldiers gathered around a fire ignoring everyone,
    everything.

    A scrawny dog barked at nothing.

        Hammers were tossed aside.

The Meeting

Only one cross had any attention.

A woman leaned hopelessly against it. One hand gripped the foot of the cross, the other arm cradled her head. I heard her sobs and I also began to weep, not knowing why.

Just to the right of the cross stood a huge centurion holding his helmet, looking up, his shoulders hung down.

Then he sunk to his knees and bowed his head. His helmet splashed in the bloody mud.

"What did they do with Yeshua?" I asked the woman.

"Do you see that sign?" She pointed a shaking finger to a crude sign nailed to the top of the cross. "Do you?" I looked up…

"They wrote it for all to see, King of the Jews, but they don't know he is their only hope."

This wasn't my question.

The soldier grabbed my coat and jerked me around. I nearly fell.

"Listen to her. Do you hear me? Listen to her."

All my life I had missed this man.

I could never explain or understand why I had to see him. Why I couldn't get him out of my mind.

Now I knew.

The angels.
    The nobles.
        The miracles.
            The scriptures.
The shouts of hosannas and hallelujahs were reserved
    for a king, this king.
The King of the Jews.
The lambs I raised all my life for sacrifice told me this
    blood, I saw on this cross, this Passover, was no ordi-
    nary blood.
I joined them on my knees, holding my staff.
    My staff holding me.
    I had done this before. I remembered.
    So long ago I asked Jehovah to save the boy Yeshua.
Now I asked Jehovah to save and forgive me for waiting
    so long.
        I wondered,
        hoping, I could explain any of this
        to Leah and the boys,
            or anyone.
That I met him,
    The perfect sacrifice.
        Born in my Bethlehem.
            Finally.
        I finally met Yeshua.

AFTERWORD

Leah and the boys were waiting at the tent.

Her face wore a peaceful look. This was a great relief. I laid my hands on the children and embraced my wife with a deeper love than ever before.

"Leah."

We had all stepped into the tent.

"Leah, boys, this tragic day is for a reason. Of this I could not be more sure. The man Yeshua may be dead, but his life is not. Just as your grandfather lives in our hearts, Yeshua should live there, too. I don't know what is next, but a soldier, a Roman soldier knew what all of Jerusalem must not have known. He knew this man was no ordinary man.

"I don't know what the future holds. I can't imagine another lamb being sacrificed after what I saw and heard today. The sign on his cross said 'King of the Jews' in three languages. It said it to me.

"We will go home tomorrow. We will tell all the family what happened here. We will do what we do the best we can, until we have a better understanding of what to do.

"I have decided that we will not sell another lamb for sacrifice." This statement brought wonder and moans from my family. I expected I would choke on those words, but I did not.

"We will sell to sustain us, but not for sacrifice. And not one lamb will pass from us until I have sat down each customer and tell them what I believe the lamb represents. I will tell them the events of this day and the events of my life that led us here. I will tell them to search as I have for what I have found.

Bethlehem, our home, was...is...the birthplace of thousands upon countless thousands of animal sacrifices. These animals were commanded by Moses to be perfect. There were to be hundreds, perhaps thousands, of sacrifices today, but I left the city by way of the altar. It was quiet. Strangely without activity. No sacrifices. No long lines. No slaughter. No fires. Nothing.

"It was as if...it was finished."

And so my reader, you must search for yourself and decide. I cannot do that for you. You have the advantage of much more information than I.

And yet,

I am quite satisfied that I have all that I need.

Bozra, child of God

REFERENCES

1.   Psalm 69:6-9 NASB

GLOSSARY

Camas	A wild field flowering plant whose white-flowered species (Deathcamas) are toxic.
Hin, hins	Jewish unit of liquid volume equal to 1/6th bath or ephath, about 2 liters.
Mantle	Ornate covering for Torah.
Omer	Jewish unit of dry measure equal to 1/10th ephah, about 3.5 liters.
Shofar	Rams horn trumpeted to call for order of worship or prayer.
Tallit	Jewish prayer shawl.
Torah	Hebrew Bible.
Tush, Tuckas	The rear end. Butt.
Wadi	A gully formed by flash floods.

WHAT OTHERS SAY

Every page put me in Bozra's sandals. Wonderful! So many thoughts, so many pictures, so many times I was Bozra. I think that says it all.
Brian Doyle

If you love Swindoll and the word pictures that Mac uses in his writing you will LOVE this book.
Dr. Larry Thompson

Mac has remarkable ability to transform one-dimensional literary characters into three-dimensional human beings.
Chaplain Robert Miller

"Forever Changed" is a book you'll want to keep to read again and again. It's a message of hope...for all of us.
Dick Kip

"Forever Changed" transposes the reader to another time. You will think about it long after you turn the last page.
Linda Sykes

As I read Mac's first book I found myself laughing out loud and then warmed to my core at his uncanny ability to draw me into each character.
Dr. Bob Barnes.

You can almost see the events happening and hear the conversations. I love it.
Sandi Powell

Other books by Mac McConnell

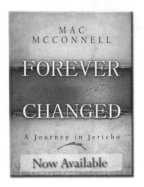

MAC MCCONNELL
FOREVER CHANGED
A Journey in Jericho
Now Available

Why would a nice Jewish boy grow up to be a despised tax collector in Jericho? And why would he go out on a limb to see the latest in a long line of would-be Messiahs?

I recommend you read—and re-read this little volume.
Terry Whalin

Mac's incredible passion burst to life in this intriguing drama.
Gigi Graham

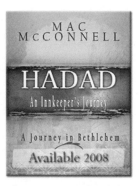

MAC MCCONNELL
HADAD
An Innkeeper's Journey
A Journey in Bethlehem
Available 2008

A famous innkeeper in Bethlehem misses a chance of a lifetime - somone more famous is born in his stable. Hadad is too busy with his paying customer to pay attention until royalty come pay a visit. He must wonder if he made the right choice.

Just as Mac brings characters to life on stage, he transforms the written word into another world…you won't want an intermission!
Janet Folger

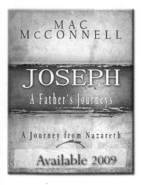

MAC MCCONNELL
JOSEPH
A Father's Journey
A Journey from Nazareth
Available 2009

The worst news a bridegroom could receive, "I'm pregnant, and the baby is not yours." Joseph, an unexpected father is faced with decisions that effect all of history.

What Mac does like no other on stage, he now does on paper. You feel as if you are living in the scene as Mac unfolds the drama, beauty and excitement of ancient history.
Tony Hammon

For book signing appearances ~ www.OneWayBooks.org ~ (954) 680-9095